W9-AOT-171

Ride Otto Ride!

For the real Otto

Atheneum Books for Young Readers
An imprint of Simon & Schuster Children's Publishing Division
1230 Avenue of the Americas
New York, New York 10020

Copyright © 2002 by David Milgrim
All rights reserved, including the right of reproduction
in whole or in part in any form.

Ready-to-Read is a registered trademark of Simon & Schuster, Inc.

Book design by Sonia Chaghatzbanian
The text for this book is set in Meta.
The illustrations for this book are rendered in digital pen-and-ink.

Printed in the United States of America
First Edition

2 4 6 8 10 9 7 5 3 1

Library of Congress Cataloging-in-Publication Data
Milgrim, David.
Ride Otto ride/ David Milgrim
p. cm.—(Ready-to-read. Pre level 1)
Summary: Otto and his friends go for a ride on an elephant.
ISBN 0-689-84417-4
[1. Robots—Fiction. 2. Elephants—Fiction.] I. Title. II. Series.
PZ7.M5955 Ri 2002
[E]—dc21   2001055335

Ride Otto Ride!

story and pictures by
DAVID MILGRIM

Atheneum Books for Young Readers
New York London Toronto Sydney Singapore

See Flip and Flop.

See Flip and Flop walk.

Walk, Flip and Flop, walk.

Walk, walk, walk,
walk, walk.

See Flip huff.
See Flop puff.

Look! Here come
Peanut and Otto.

See Flip and Flop ride.

Ride, Flip and
Flop, ride.

Look, there is Skip.

See Skip ride.
See Flip and Flop ride.

See Otto ride.
Ride, everyone, ride.

Look, here are
Al, Sal, Hal, and Val.
Hop on up!

See Peanut go.
Go, Peanut, go.

Look, there is Spec.
See Spec hop on too.

See Otto bang.

Bang, bang, bang!

See Peanut ride.
Ride, Peanut, ride!